CONCEALMENT

**Story and Art by
Alex Cockburn**

"Concealment" by Alex Cockburn (a. k. a. Ookami Kemono)
Editor: Tsunami Woodside
Contact Alex Cockburn at GothicKemono@aol.com
www.furaffinity.net/user/o-kemono

A special thank you to everyone who supported me:

Tsunami, Christina, Charlene, Joe, Eric, Matthew, GamerKitty, Chris, Panda, Ben, LightLion, Samantha, Angela, Valery, Sarah, Elisha, and all my fur friends!

A very special thanks to:
Mom, Dad, and Elana

Published by Rabbit Valley® Comics
www.rabbitvalley.com

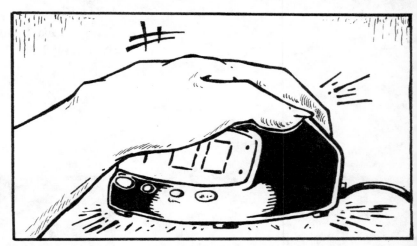

Monday... Febuary 9th...7 am...
For some reason, I feel that there was no weekend at all... It just flew by...

And now I've got less than an hour to get dressed and go to work; to abandon the warm bed and move my tired body...

Floppers is on the floor, a bad sign. Whenever he's there I know it's going to be a bad day...

THUD!

YO.OH!

Already, I feel like shit and wish that night will come so I can go back to bed...

Sorry it took so long...

SSSiiiGGGHHH

You met Dan at the rave dance. You put on this "costume" and acted really differently. You basically lied to him about yourself just to get him to like you and hang out with you. You moved and spoke differently in front him him, I mean I almost didn't reconize you myself...

You even put on pump-up bra and wore a thong...

But then something happened between you two. You called me after we split up from the club in a nervous state. You didn't tell me what had happened....

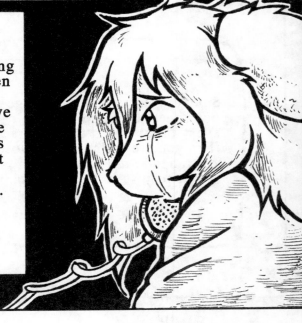

You never went into detail about it. You kept me guessing through the night. Samsy, what really happened?

He just broke up with me and I overreacted on the phone. That was about it...

Listen, I have to go and get changed back for work. Tonight is "Goth-Punk" Night at the club and I have to get ready.

"Goth-Punk" Night? Do you plan to get dressed up and act like a depressed and isolated person to get attention?

Any difference...?

Samsy...Why do you do this to yourself? Every time you go out to clubs, you go as someone else. It's like you don't know who you really are...

You're really scaring me and I worry about you.

Shit...Where is it?
Where's my collar...

CLICK

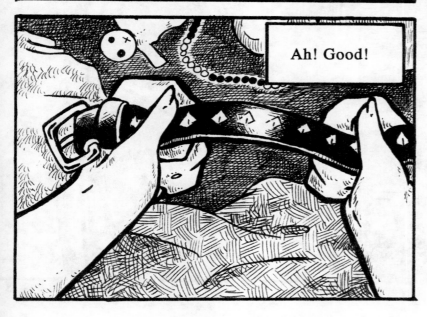

Ah! Good!

Wow. A long line tonight.

Why am I feeling so nervous about this? I've never been to a "goth-punk" club before. There are so many here who are more styled up than me...

...WHAT...

That's it. Keep in character!

Dancing, drinking, partying, social gatherings: this is what this club is all about. Those full of energy can get up and dance or do crazy activities. The lonely, quiet types, the ones waiting for someone to come and join them, can sit and drink at the bar.

CRUNCH

Jewels, fishnet, piercings, hair and fur gel... those people know how to dress like real punks and goths. It's all about looks and how people dress. They seem to blend into the crowd easier than those who know that they aren't as cool as others...

And here I am, still dressed in my work shirt, with a canine collar: the only thing that makes me "punk-ish". Who would want to pay attention to me? All I can do now is try just to act depressed and quiet.

...WHAT...

The only lass alone at the bar, eating small nuts and no male. Where is your mate?

I don't have one, and don't bother me or my nuts...

Five "Red Death" drinks, sir.

Cheers, just put it on my tab.

Stop your sulking and come and get drunk with me and my group. We have room for more breasts your size.

A group huh? A small cluster of people who would kick me out at first sight?

Bollocks! You're alone at the bar on monday night. You don't look like the type to sit around and eat nuts. I'm the leader of my group and they'll accept anyone I bring over. So take those bloody shells out of your mouth and come over!

Hey! BarBoy! Make one more drink for me!

Get your ass up and come and join us at the end!

Someone is interested in me, even though he has a thick British mouth. That happened so quickly! What would his friends think of me? How will my first impression come out?

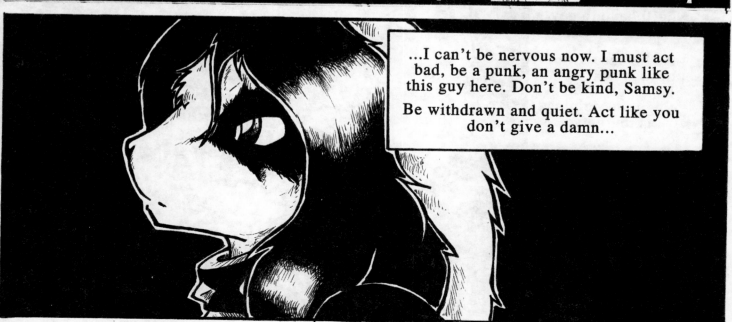

...I can't be nervous now. I must act bad, be a punk, an angry punk like this guy here. Don't be kind, Samsy.

Be withdrawn and quiet. Act like you don't give a damn...

Well, what brings you guys over to this club tonight?

Does Jimmy just take you out to anywhere he feels?

Something like that. We are not dressed up in what we usually wear since this mouse here stained our clothes with his last drunken outburst.

GOLP!

HEY! I love my drinks and I'll act any way I want when I'm drunk! At bars, all I care about are booze and big tits!

...ok...?

DRINK UP AND JOIN OUR SCREWED UP GROUP!

Ugh...

Ow...My head...
Where am I?

...I'm home... Is it morning?

What happened last night?
When did I get back?

I'm still in my work clothes.
I can feel that collar on
my neck and gel in my hair.

Yuck...
I smell like coffee and
beer.

Shit... My head! So this is what a "hang-over" feels like... Geeze...

RING RING RING

HELLO...?

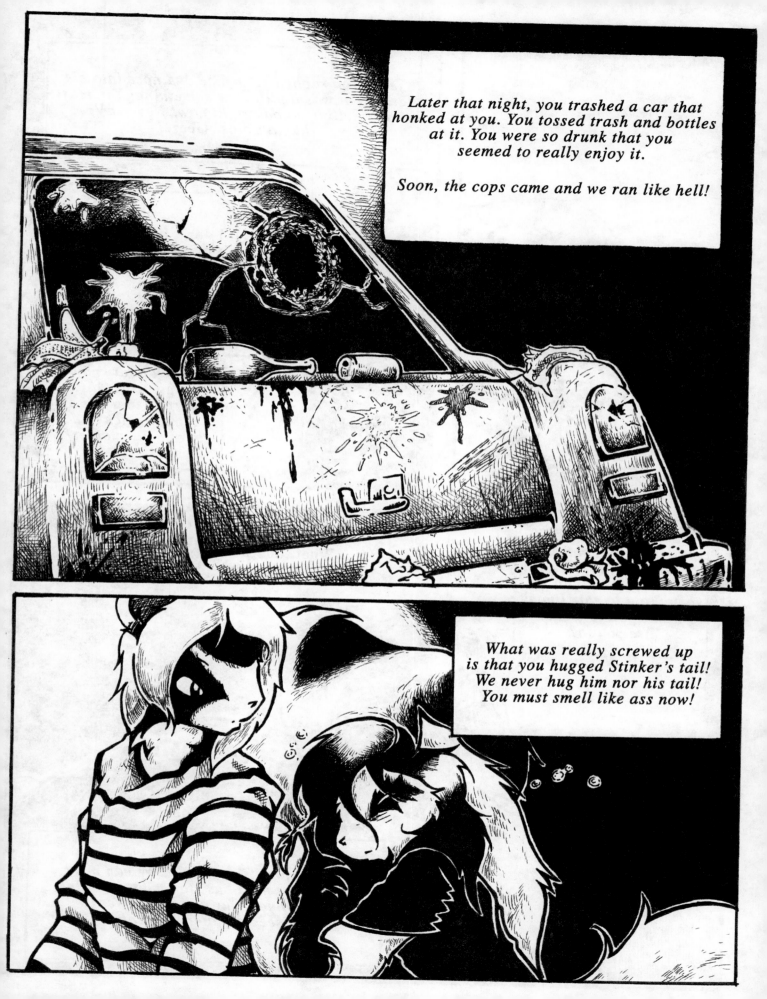

56-58 BUS
9 AM - MIDNIGHT

TUESDAY
FEB 10TH
50¢

Su

102-05106 8 FT 19"

CLINK
CLINK
BEEP!

95¢

Second day with these new "friends". From last night, it seems that I have gained their interest and respect. The thing is, I dont know anything about these punks: only their names.

I had to wear my work clothes again, along with my chain and collar. I bet the others will have much better outfits than me.

Oh well. I can get more clothes at the mall when I get the chance. This will give me a chance to update my closet and dresser...

Oh god! What about Sasha! I hugged his tail last night! I can't believe that I did that! What if he is pissed off at me for doing that?!

He's kind of cute. He's not as mean as the others...

I can't be weak now. I need to be tough and rude in order for me to blend into this group without trouble.

Just relax.
Don't freeze up now.

THE PRU. MALL

Why did you change your hair and not your face?

You what? You've got a mouth on you, Nut-eater!

SHIT! Calm down, both of you. I don't care WHO smells like ass or who looks like shit. I'm here to shop, ok? Stinker is waiting for us at the game store.

Yeah, maybe he can send this grotty hybrid to the clothing shop to get something more interesting...

So... about last night...

Elisha told me that you don't remember what happened. Is that true?

I guess I drank too much last night. Elisha filled me in on the details.

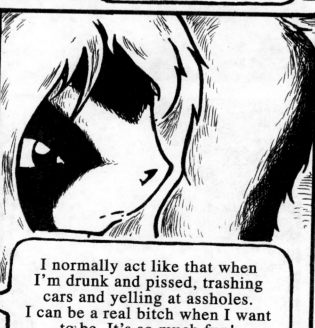

I normally act like that when I'm drunk and pissed, trashing cars and yelling at assholes. I can be a real bitch when I want to be. It's so much fun!

Heh, yeah. You really went out! I'd never seen anyone act that crazy before except for Jimmy. I never thought that someone like you would cause so much damage.

THE SPIKED COLLAR

This place is pretty amazing for extreme trinkets and jokes. I wonder if I should buy something just to impress Stinker and Jimmy instead of for myself.

Should I get some creepy looking dolls for my room...

....or should I just get "suggestive" shirts that are not my taste?

Maybe some hardcore books about magic and vampires?

Jimmy said anything sexy. I wouldn't mind that myself. So why don't you just pick something. I will be waiting here for you, ok?

Fine.

Magazine and photo cutouts are plastered all over this wall, each one featuring attractive-looking females: general fashion tips, "how to please your mate", those kinds of rambling articles. I remember seeing these the last time I was here - I picked up a few of those dating tips.

He said "sexy and cool". What is that to him? I don't know what those are by myself; I thought the outfits I got last time were sexy and cool, but I guess that's all in the eye of the beholder. I just hope that I don't come out looking like a fool or a poser to others.

Everybody hates posers...

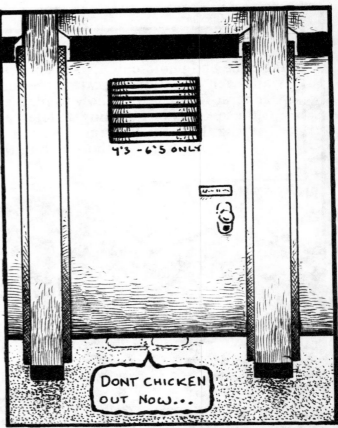

Well... I managed to pick up something that Stinker and, hopefully, Jimmy likes. This will burn a hole in my wallet, but it's for the best.

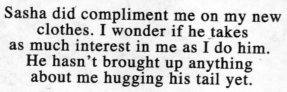

Sasha did compliment me on my new clothes. I wonder if he takes as much interest in me as I do him. He hasn't brought up anything about me hugging his tail yet.

Jason really seems to like her. Even though he is drunk and stupid, he has a pretty good judgement of character.

SERIOUSLY, DO YOU EVER SHUT YOUR GOB, YOU TWAT!?

Nut-eater doesn't act like me at all! Got it?! She's too quiet and not to mention thick! It's almost like she's a poser, like she is only pretending to be something they are not! Fakes just wind me up, ok?!

Will you relax?! Shit! Nut-eater is not a poser at all. If she was, she wouldn't have done all that shit last night! She's like April: quiet but she can bare her claws when she really needs to.

Just chill the hell out, and give her a god-damn chance, ok Jimmy?!

Give her a chance, ok? If you want to help her not be a "poser" then teach her a thing or two.

I'm no ones bloody teacher, especially not to stupid bints, but if it will help her not be such a joke, then I will show her how to bare her teeth and claws...

HEY.

LICK EM

Sorry that we're late. We just went browsing around the mall.

Hey, Nut-eater! Looking sharp there with the skull shirt! Very nice!

It's strange. I don't think I got Sasha's attention at all. It was almost like he was just rolling his eyes at me and my new outfit. All he pointed out was the lack of room in my shirt...

Jimmy didn't say a thing at all, except insults. Maybe that's his way of saying "nice clothes"? Should I try harder with Sasha and see if he's interested in me? But why am I even thinking about this?! I just wanted to join their group: nothing else. Why am I thinking so much about Sasha?

That horse seems familiar in some way..

Wait! I know!

He was the same one who was checking me out outside the club!

I see you are checking me out, just like last night!

What is it?!

You got something to say? Do you have a problem? Stop looking at me or I'll rip your balls off, ya damn pony!

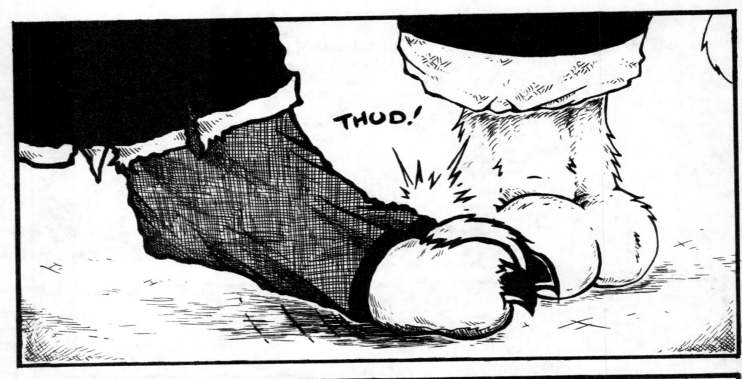

Heh! You are nothing but a short punk wannabe, just trying to pick a fight!

Why don't you go play with a ball of yarn and be with your mommy, you British pussy!

OOOH CRAP

Care to repeat that...?

Too much fluff in your ears, kitten? I said you go back to your...

Come on! Get up! Speak louder this time, hyena!!

Hey, if you are through playing "teacher", you should run like hell before security catches you!

Fine... NUT-EATER! Shape yourself up, get that shit off of your clothes and go home!

Grow some fangs in that weak jaw of yours and learn to fight back, got it?!

Hey, why don't you come to my place so you don't have to walk home with cheese on your tits and get teased again. My place is only a few stops away from here.

Your place?

Yeah, a few blocks away. You don't have to, but it will save you from embarrassment.

If not, feel free to walk home like that.

Um, sure. What the hell...

Awesome. Put your trash away and get your old clothes by the table. I'll wait for you here.

His place? Oh god, I said "sure"? How am I supposed to act? What are we going to do there? Maybe be wants me to change my clothes there? Maybe in front of him...?

Maybe he will help me undress... Maybe he's a very tender guy... Soft fur, warm breath... Maybe he'll accept me for who and what I am.

Why am I thinking about this? He's so hot, so cute... He seems to be the kind of guy who would act slow and gentle instead of fast and hard...

I just want to see what kind of punks she was hanging with today.

I wanted you guys to piss her friends off just to see how dangerous they are...

Look, jackass, I got bit on the face because of this! You'll pay us DOUBLE or I'll rip your head off and shove it down the toilet!

Listen, I don't know who you are, but do your own spying from now on. If I ever see your face around here or in my sight ever again, I won't hesitate to picture that British feline's face on your body and rip your guts out!

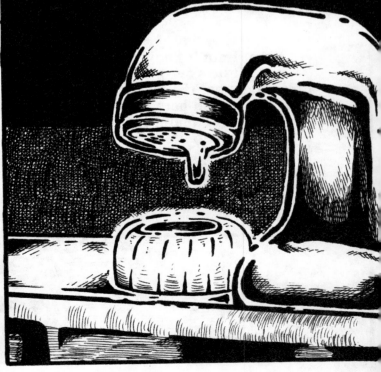

Here.

The bathroom is down the hall. Go and get yourself cleaned up.

What am I doing? Here, in his home? Am I *that* crazy?
How should I act? What does he think of me?
Does he have an interest in me? Am I really his type?
Why am I trying to so hard to try to please him and get him
to notice me? It's like begging for a toy from your parents...

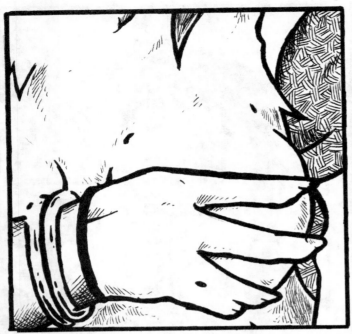

I forgot about those. I pretended they were bigger by a whole cup size for a while at least.

It's all about the body for males. The breast size... It's like that's all males want. I dont have a great body but I still want him...

Flop

EVODAT

Great, now I'm catching myself just staring at the bathroom door...
How pathetic...

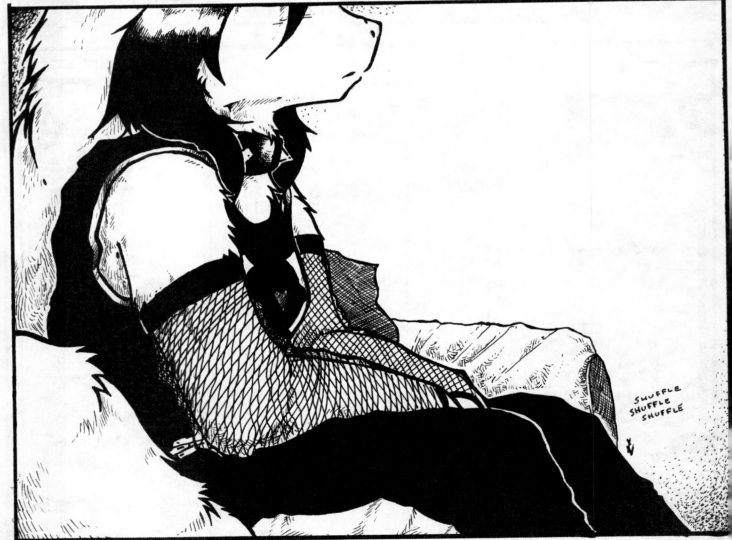

That reminds me: I don't have any punk or heavy metal music in my place. I should pick up some later today...

KNOCK KNOCK

Who could that be...?

Jason?

Well well, if it isn't the well-developed Nut-eater! What are you doing here? Sniffing under the skunk's tail now, are we?

You have a big mouth for someone who is wearing demonic boxers in the middle of the hallway. Now I *have* seen everything!

Well, if you don't like them, I guess I can just slide these guys down~

YOU BETTER KEEP THOSE ON, YOU ASS!

I'm going to get changed and then Jason and I are going to hang out at his place upstairs. Why don't you go home and grow some fangs for the next fight you get into. Try to find something sexy to wear for the party, ok?

You should try to find something that doesn't cover the underside of your tail, baby~!

ASSHOLE!

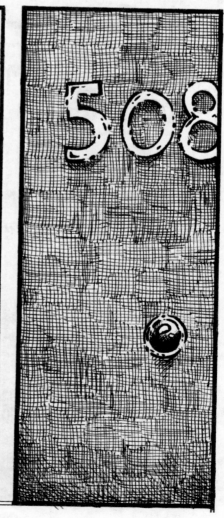

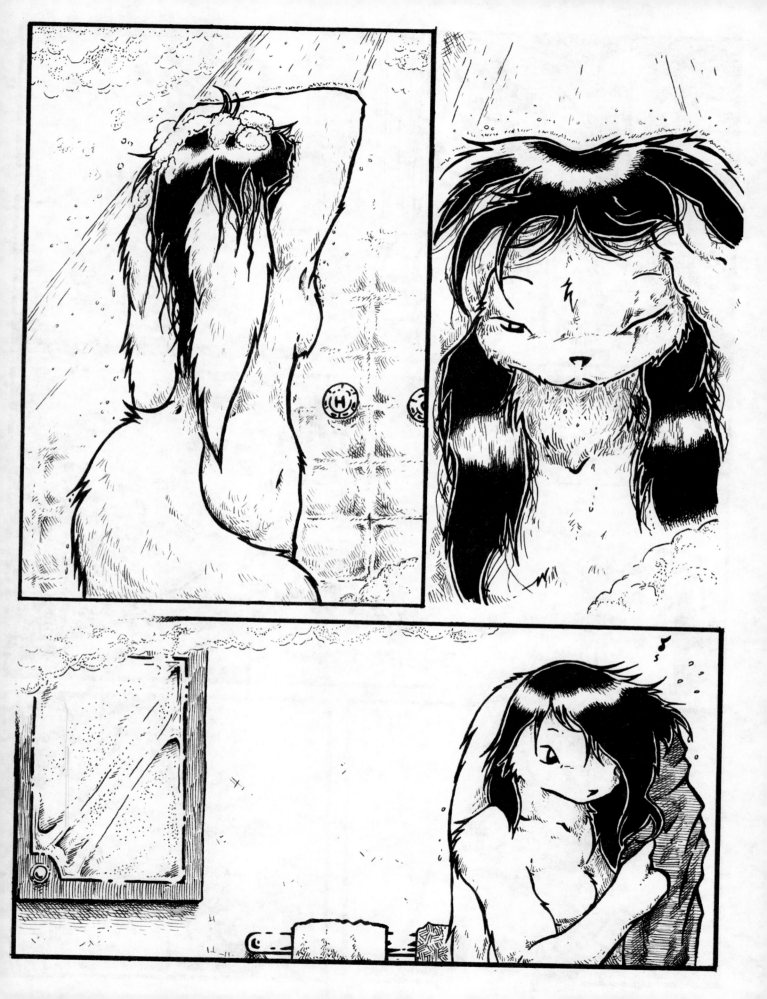

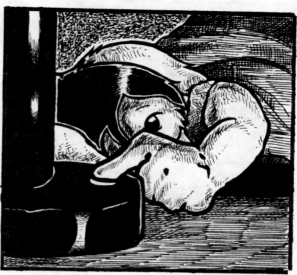

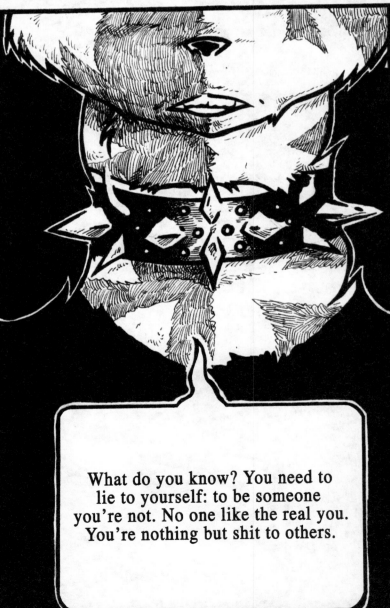

OW! OW!
Sasha!

YOU ARE STILL NOTHING BUT A LYING FAKE!

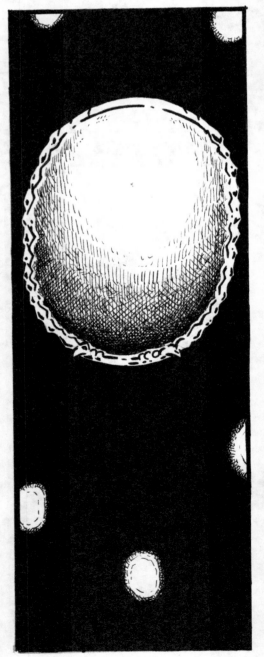

So, I told her about the party. She wants to come.

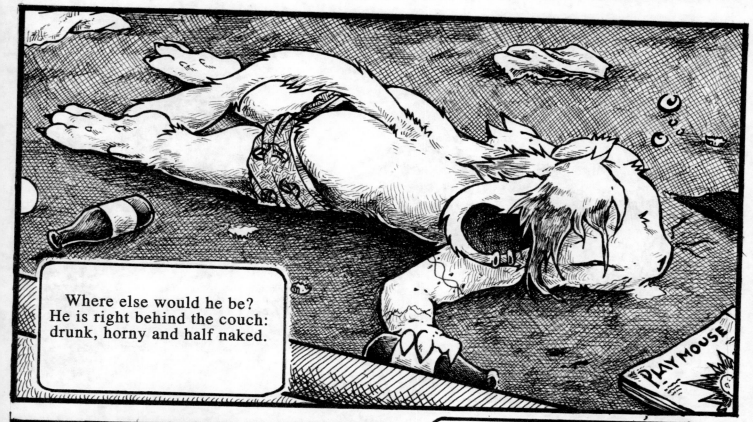

Where else would he be?
He is right behind the couch:
drunk, horny and half naked.

Well, slap him on the arse or kick
him in the face. Wake him up!
I want the little shit mouse to
entertain me while I'm plastered!

Ok! Ok! Relax! Go have another
beer or something... sheesh!

HEY! EARTH TO THE STRIPED PIECE OF CRAP! HELLO~! Didn't you hear me, stinker?! Do you have any spray paint?!

Huh? Why?

To paint some damn cars and walls, maybe your bloody stupid mush! Get the cans and any beer Jason has left in the fridge! Next, get your head OUT OF YOUR ARSE!!

I do see a change in the way she acts. Every time she's with the group, she becomes very violent...

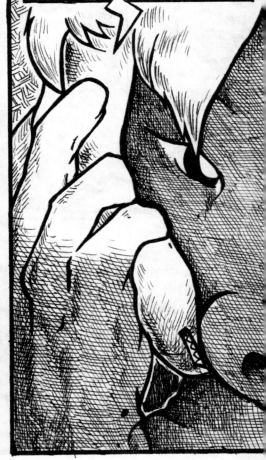

From what you told me earlier today, the way you discribed her, that doesn't sound anything like the Samantha I know...

She seems to be getting much influence from the British feline. After the fight, he seemed to be teaching her how to defend herself the next time she is bullied...

She was always a pushover over the years... She's the last hybrid you would expect to show her fangs...

If she's being taught how to fight from a violent person, that makes me worried about what kind of person she's becoming...

...sniff...

Do you want me to come over?

No no... I'm fine. I'm ok, I'm just really worried about Samantha. I think she is in trouble...

Listen, I am greatful that you are doing this for me. She would have spotted me if I was spying on her... You are a great friend.

Thank you very much...

No problem. I want to be a detective one day, so this "spying" thing is good practice and it helps me with my studies.

Speaking of which, I need to get back to the books. I have a lot of homework to catch up on. I will call you tomorrow to check up on you, ok?

Ok. Have a good night...

×CLICK×

* CLICK *

SEE YOU AT FUNLAND

Dear Diary,

I'm sorry that I have not written to you in a while, but I have been very busy and have been hanging out with the gang. As you know, I am slowly trying to blend in with the group and trying to get Sasha's attention. The more I hang out with him, the more attracted I feel towards him. He is more appealing than any other male I have been with. He is interesting and kind. I have also changed a lot ever since I was accepted into Jimmy's gang...

I have been shopping for new clothes: trying to find something that would make Sasha eyeball me. I haven't just been shopping for shirts and pants but also some kinky underwear to match my outfits and style. The constant spending really put a hole in my wallet. The gang still drags me around. We go out to lunch and to clubs. Now and then, when we are drunk out of our fur, we cause chaos and mischief around the city and we've always got away with it. Jimmy has been teaching me how to defend myself and to fight dirty for the next time I'm pushed around. He's very violent and aggressive, but he has had his share of fighting over the years...

After a while, April came back to the group. She doesn't talk that much...in fact she seems to completely ignore everyone for some reason... Sasha says that she is just the quiet type. I used to be like her when I was younger. April seems to spend close time with Sasha. I can't help but feel jealous...

Work is still hell for me. I can't wear my punk outfit there or I might get fired. I'm not happy at this job, but it pays my rent and everything else I need to get by...

I also spent most of my time shopping for Sasha. It's going to be Valentines Day tomorrow and I want to give him something special, but I had to find something that wasn't too cute... and you know how I love cute things...

SQWEAK!

I know I lie to him every time I see him about who I am, but I worked hard to become something that he likes and I don't want to lose it. I have been avoiding my friends because of my new persona. I don't want them to be involved with my matters.
I don't know who I am. That's why I'm doing this — to try to find myself and who I am. It is a silly thing, I know, but I want to know who I am and what I am...
I love Sasha. I really do. I just hope he will feel the same way...

I am going to see him at the mall later today to give him his small gift.

Not really, no... You seem a little over-dressed there. You can't resist the temptation to wear those sweaters.

Hey, Nut-eater. Have you been waiting long?

Hey, I like sweaters, so shut up. What is in the bag? Did Jimmy tell you to bring anything?

No, he didn't. What is in yours?

Oh, just a few things for April. She told me to pick her up some things. You don't mind if she tags along with us today, right?

Oh... no, I don't mind.

What's wrong with you?!

Nothing. I was hoping that we could just hang out together.

Why?

I don't know... We didn't really hang out that long at your place a few days ago. And whenever we see each other you always have the gang around, and I was just hoping that it could be you and me today...

Geeze! You make it sound like we're dating or something! Why do you want to just be alone with me all the time? What are you hiding from me?

Um... well... I...

Relax.

... STUPID ...

Why doesn't she answer
my emails anymore...?

Hey, it's me. I'm just wondering if you have anything about Samsy...

Oh, I'm sorry Becky... I've been busy with school work...

I'm sorry... I should have known. Do you want me to leave you alone and call you later tonight?

No no. I need a break anyway. You sound a little down, Becky. What is it?

I just can't get a hold of Samsy. She isn't responding to my emails or calls. It has been a few days and I can't get through to her. I was just hoping that you would have something to report...

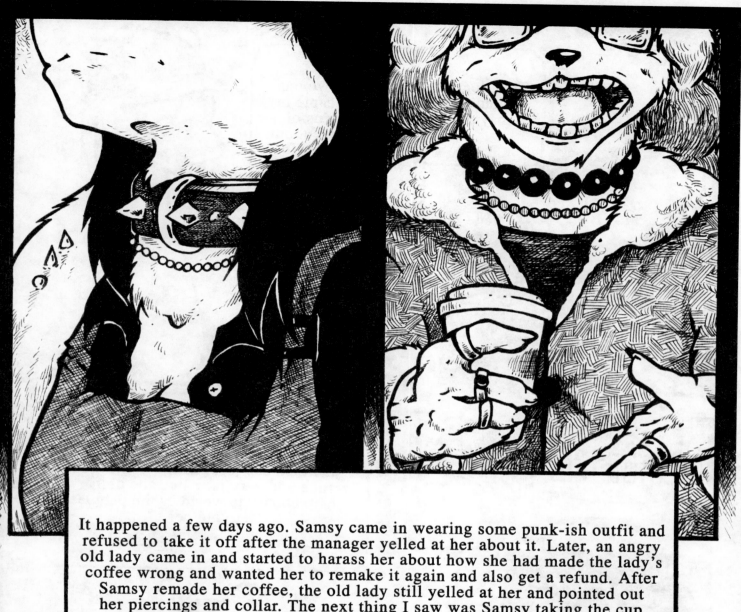

It happened a few days ago. Samsy came in wearing some punk-ish outfit and refused to take it off after the manager yelled at her about it. Later, an angry old lady came in and started to harass her about how she had made the lady's coffee wrong and wanted her to remake it again and also get a refund. After Samsy remade her coffee, the old lady still yelled at her and pointed out her piercings and collar. The next thing I saw was Samsy taking the cup of coffee from the lady and tossing it in her face. There was soon a fight and the manager fired Samsy on the spot before the woman could say that she'd sue the café.

Hey, have you guys seen Nut-eater?

Yeah stud, she is right over there...

I demand a reason! You left the mall without saying anything to me! I spent most of my time looking all over the place for you! You didn't return my calls, you ignore me and treat me like shit! You were never like this to me before!

FINE! Here is your reason! You are a thick-headed, sweater-fetish, stripe-tailed son of a bitch skunk!! You just piss me off whenever I look at you!

Jimmy has taught me a lot – like not taking shit from others, like you! You disgust me, skunk! Just your presence makes me want to vomit! Why don't you do us a favor and get out of our group and die, you smelly, striped load of shit!

What the hell is with all the yelling! I could hear the bloody racket in the next room!!

STINKER TRIED TO RAPE ME! HE ATTACKED ME!

Woh! Woh! This is not-!

You're out of the gang Sticker! If I see you again, I will bury you twenty feet in the ground!!

Nut-eater, come on. This wanker is about to leave. He won't bother you again...

65/51 BUS

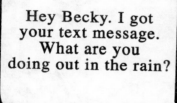

Hey Becky. I got your text message. What are you doing out in the rain?

Woh, Becky. What's the matter? What happened to you today...?

Becky, please talk to me.
What is going on? Why did
you call me? You sounded
so distraught...

It's Samsy. I went to her place today to talk to her...

The way she spoke to me on the intercom made me worried about her...

When I was at her door, she acted very uptight, it was almost like she hated me for some reason. Behind her was this rude, British punk. He mouthed off to me and told Samsy what to say and do. It was like he wanted her to hate me and she was obeying him without question...

When I tried to tell her how I was worried about her, she yelled at me, telling me that she doesn't need me anymore. She acted like I was her enemy and tossed me out of her life. She never spoken to me like that before...

She kicked me out, telling me that she never wants to see me again. I cried in the rain and called you...

She shut me out completely! She treated me like I was nothing! Why is she like this?! That was not Samsy in that apartment!

Listen Becky... I have to tell you something... Remember you asked about that skunk that was with her?

His name is Sasha. I think he was the one who sent her over the edge. I saw him kissing a girl and I guess Samsy saw it and cracked.

I'm tired of guys toying with her. I'm going to end this and I don't want you standing in my way!

That's him...

Listen, I don't know who...

SAMANTHA! The punk hybrid! My friend, you bastard!

Hybrid?

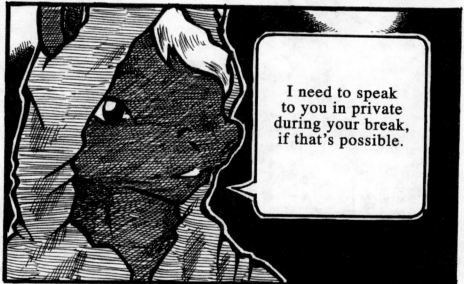

I need to speak to you in private during your break, if that's possible.

My break is in an hour. I just want to know what the hell is going on here. You come in here and assault me! I could have called the manager and tossed you both out!

Yes, and I *am* sorry for that... We can meet you in the café down the street.

Becky, let's go...

... So, that is how Samsy felt about me... I didn't even know her real name...

I know that love is confusing. Some see it easier than others. She showed it multiple times to you from what I have seen, not to mention changing her personallity and physical appearance. When you broke her heart in the mall with that small "misunderstanding", she snapped and lost her trust in everyone. The only people she could turn to are those punks who tell her what to do, even though they treat her like shit...

I just can't believe that she had feelings for me: a skunk. I guess I too was blinded by her flirtations. I never wanted to hurt her, but that night...

From what you told me from that fight, I never expected her to be attacked by Dan. It's terrible, my god... Sam has been trying to be part of a group for years and it's been nothing but one drama after the other. She needs help. She needs someone to take care of her and watch her. I'm scared for Samsy. I fear for the worse...

... My god...

... I want her back...

...SNIFF...

Becky, I will try to help her: talk to her. I've never been in this situation before, but I will try...

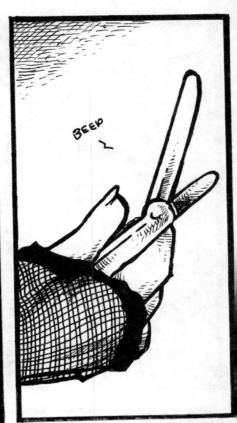

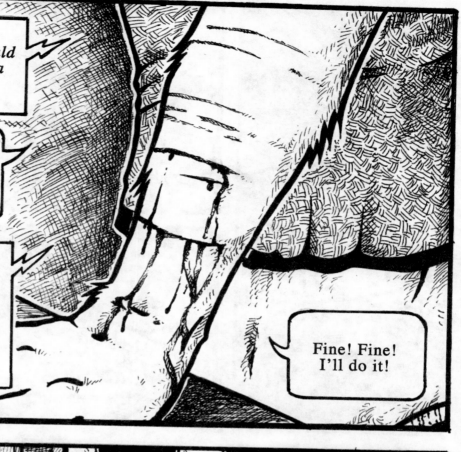

What the shit?! I told you I would give you money if I could get a shag off you last night!

I told you... I'm not in the mood to be "shagged" by anyone right now...

Well GET IN THE MOOD!! Go get the paint and beer, ok? I don't care how you do it: pay or steal. Get in the bloody mood and lift up your tail next time I see you, or you are out of the gang, ok?! Bitch.

Fine! Fine! I'll do it!

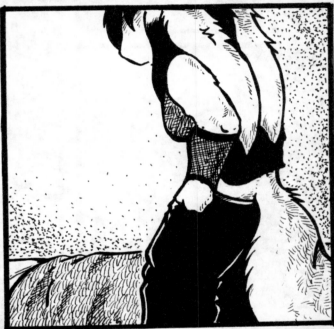

Well, don't just
stand there!
Tell me what you
want and get out
of my sight, Stinker!

Listen Sam, your
friend Becky is very
worried about you...

She told me your
address so I can come
and talk to you...

Why am I even bothering talking to you?! You attacked me last time we spoke! I should just rip your tail off right here and now! Jimmy taught me a few of his own fighting moves so I know WHERE to strike and HOW to make you bleed!

I am sorry for that night, but—

OH SHUT UP! Yeah, right... sure you are sorry. Have pity for the hybrid! Everyone pities the hybrid because we always get shit on for our mixed features! We are lost and confused pieces of shit who don't know what we are or who we are! You will never understand...

Sam, listen. I'm not really 100% skunk...

HUH..?

What the hell does that mean?! You're making fun of me again aren't you?! If that's your game, you can just jump right out the damn window and die!

I'm in no mood to be tossed around by anyone right now! I had a bad day today and I'm ready to stick my claws into anyone who pisses me off right now!

Becky told me about you pulling a false act of being a punk girl! She told me that you are really a nice girl who is trying to fit into a bad crowd just to be noticed!

She told me a lot about you. She told me that you dress up as someone you are not, just to try to fit in with any group. You act so differently around others and you even ignore your friends who are trying to show concern for you...

This is not you. This isn't who you are, Sam.

You are not a punk girl. You are not a violent person. Stop pretending to be something that you are not...

Stinker, you don't know me at all... You don't...

No Sam, I do know you. You just proved to me that you can't do something against your nature. You don't need to act like this anymore...

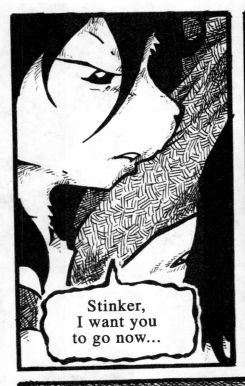

Stinker,
I want you
to go now...

Samantha, I have
deep feelings for you.

I know it seems fast but I was blind to
your flirtations in the past until now.
No one has had feelings like this for
me as much as you and *that* means a lot
to me...Everytime I look into your
eyes, my feelings for you grow

stronger – so strong
that I can't just
ignore them
anymore...

I want you, Sam.

I was a fool, Sam. I treated
you unfairly. I need someone
like you in my life.
Please, be yourself tonight.
Be Samantha for me for a while.
Don't pretend you are
a punk girl, please...

Stinker, I'm
sorry that I was
so rude...

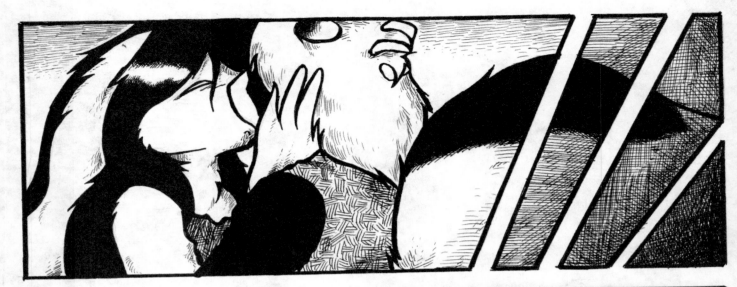

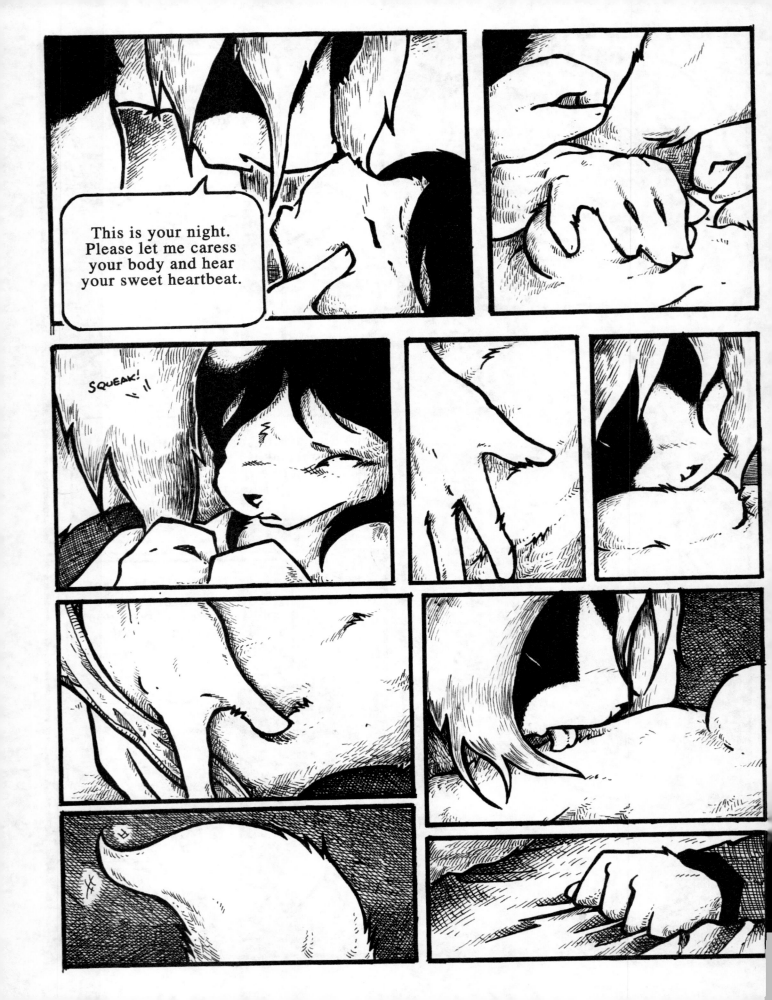

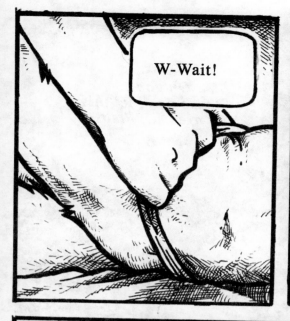

W-Wait!

Do you want me to stop, Samsy?

No, no! ... Um, I'm just... after what happened on my last "date", I'm just... not ready yet...

I know that you and April are together, I don't want to come between you two...

Sam, I plan to leave my pants on all night for you. April is just a friend to me: nothing more. You are my first, Sam. You can trust me...

Like I said, this night is only about you...

Good morning.

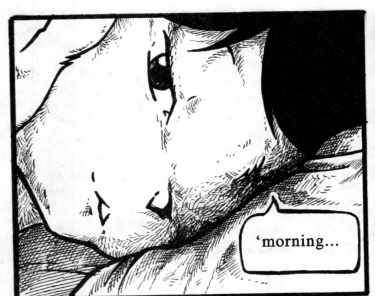

'morning...

Did you sleep well?

mm... move over...

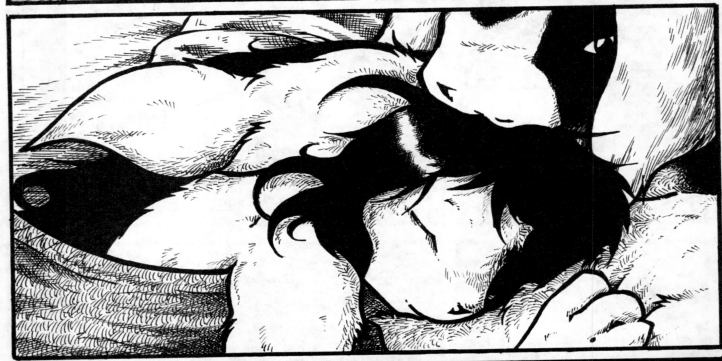

Last night you squeaked, mewed whimpered and panted. I tried to guess what spieces you are...

Hehe!

Sasha, I have a question...

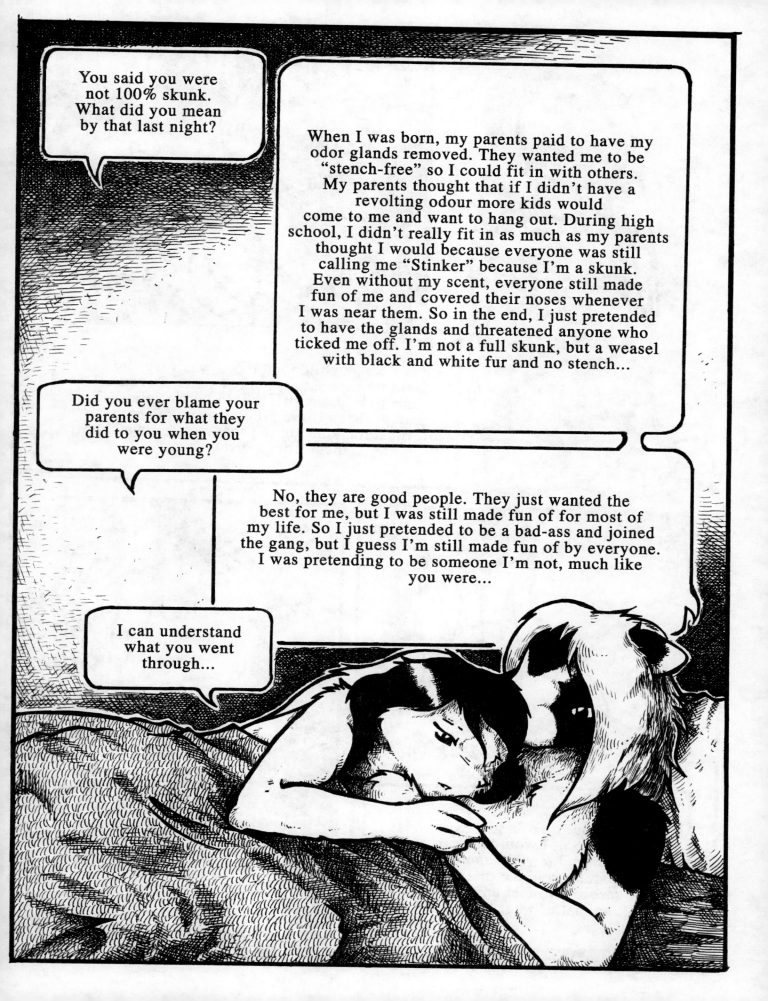

I had a rough childhood too. I was very shy and timid throughout my school years. Because I was a hybrid, no girls would let me join their groups: even if the group was mixed breed. So I just remained in the shadows and watched them from a distance...

I was made fun of a lot. Every day after school, I would sulk in my room and feel terrible about myself. My parents told me that hybrids are rare and to feel unique about myself, no matter what they might say.

That's easier said than done...

I've tried joining groups and gangs. I've been hurt and tossed around so many times. Then I joined you guys and... well, I just gave up and didn't mind being pushed around by Jimmy and the others. I almost lost all touch with myself because of the abuse.

Have you and Jimmy ever shared the same bed before?

No. Jimmy is brash, harsh and very violent. In many ways, he is like Dan. If I wasn't cold-hearted, I would have broken down. I kept my tail down in front of him. We are not close at all. We fight almost all the time.

Leave Jimmy. Leave the gang. You don't need them. You don't need to be hurt by them anymore...

I don't know. I've finally found a group that has accepted me and I don't want to have that taken away...

This group is not for you at all, Sam. These cuts on your arm are proof that they are hurting you both mentally and physically.

I was like you. I needed a group to fit into: a place where I felt like I was accepted by others. That was a mistake. I am better off not being in Jimmy's shadow.

You don't need them. They're not your friends. They use you for their pleasure. Jimmy is just using you as another tail to hump. Did you know that Elisha used to be his girlfriend? But he's not happy with just having one girl to screw around with.

April is mute. I see a lot of her in you. She wants to fit in and feel accepted by others. I helped her get into that group when I joined. Sooner or later she'll leave the group too, like us, but that is only when she's ready to.

I think it's amazing that half of group are just people wanting to try to fit into something...

.. SNIFF ..

I will leave them just to be with you...

This is taking too bloody long! What time is it?! Where the hell is Nut-eater?!

It's around noon time... She's never late to see us.

GILO

That stupid bint! She was supposed to be here by now with beer and paint! I told her to bring them last night!

Keep your collar on. Maybe the bus is late. Why the hell are you so concerned about her anyways, Jimmy?!

Why don't you shut your gob...?

I heard that Nut-eater pushed away Jimmy's sexual advances. He really wants to get his nose under her tail! Jimmy with a hybrid! HA! That is really something new to see! But I don't blame him at all!

Her breasts are big, her ass is firm and that face just wants to be covered with your–

One more word out of your mouth, you prat, and I will shove that magazine up your dick!

So, it sounds like you have a crush on her, huh?

Arseholes...

All you gave her were bad dreams and scars. You treated her like trash and talked crap behind her back! You are no friend to her at all!

We have had enough of your temper and foul mouth, Jimmy!

We were never going to be together, Jimmy. Sasha is the one I'm with. He's someone that you will never be. Do yourself a favor and get some help!

CARE TO REPEAT THAT ...?

Thank you... for defending me from Jimmy.

It really pissed me off that he placed his hands on you like that and then smacked you. You did well yanking his whiskers off...

I wanted to do that for a long time. I just didn't want to face him alone.

You called him "Dan", Samsy. Did you mean to call him that?

It just slipped out, but I guess him and Dan are out of my life now. I want to start over...

Sasha, why do you love me?

You are kind, honest and respectful. You are very cute and sweet. I love you because you're unique.

Why do you love me, Samsy?

You respect me, you protected me and you saved me from Jimmy. You don't treat me like anyone else ever has. You're not abusive and mean. I would feel lost without you.

...and I... I think that skunks are sexy because they are unique too...

I think you are just cute.

Well, I need to go back home and clean. Then I've got a personal errand to go do: to try to fix something I broke a while ago. Then, after that, spend the night with you at my place. Maybe tomorrow I will look for another job since I lost my last one.

So, what are we going to do now?

Maybe, tonight,
you can sleep without
your pants on...?

How about dinner
then a movie first?
Like a real date first?

That sounds
like a good idea.

Let me walk you to
the bus just in case
Jimmy is looking
for you, ok?

Thank you,
Sasha.

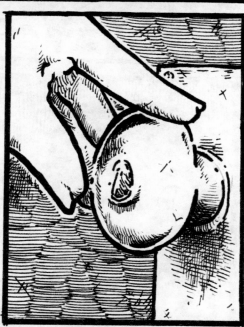

Yes...?

Samantha?

Becky, I'm here, wondering if you would accept an apology from a stupid punk girl who hurt your feelings and our friendship...?

THE END